Roundabout Train

Story by Betty Ren Wright

Pictures by Charles Clement

WHITMAN and TELL-A-TALE are registered trademarks of
Western Publishing Company, Inc

142

A WHITMAN BOOK
Western Publishing Company, Inc.
Racine, Wisconsin

Tinytown stood at the bottom of a tall thin hill. Railroad tracks ran out from it on every side, just like the prickles of a porcupine.

Some of the tracks went up and over the tall thin hill. Some of them went around the tall thin hill. Only the very oldest steam engine had followed them all.

"Tomorrow a big yellow diesel engine is coming to Tinytown," said the old fellow one night. "We will have to teach him the ins and outs and roundabouts of Tinytown."

"Too-too-tomorrow!" tooted the other steam engines. "Hope he's nice, hope he's nice!"

Early the next morning, as the sun crept over the tall thin hill, there came a whistle and a roar outside Tinytown.

"There he is!" chugged the oldest steam engine. "Get ready to toot a cheery hello."

The roar grew louder. The whistle grew louder. The big yellow diesel whooshed into town.

"Clear the tracks, clear the tracks, get out of my way, old clickety-clacks," he howled. "I'm big and strong, I'm never wrong, clear the tracks for *meeeeeeeee!*"

The steam engines listened. They chugged sadly and turned away.

"Too-too-too noisy," tooted one.

"And too-too-too boasty," tooted another.

Even the oldest engine turned away without saying hello.

"Too-too-too bad," he tooted softly. "He'll have to be taught a lesson."

That afternoon a long string of
freight cars was pushed into the
yard. Tank cars and flat cars, coal
cars and cattle cars rattled and
roared in a row.

"This is the longest train we've ever had," said the yardmaster. "We'll let the new yellow diesel pull it."

"Yes-yes-yes," hissed the big diesel. "I can do it better than any of these old clickety-clacks."

The steam engines watched as he hustled to the front of the train, pushing the other locomotives out of his way.

"Terrible manners!" they tooted. "Too-too-too bad!"

The oldest engine chugged, so softly that no one else heard him, "Yes, sir, he'll have to be taught a lesson."

What a heavy load that long train was! The diesel tugged and

he pulled. He whistled and he howled. At last the train began to move.

"Which way, which way?" called the big yellow diesel. "Which way shall I go?"

And before anyone else could answer, the oldest steam engine said, "When you get to the first switch, go left."

The long train moved faster. Sparks flickered from the great wheels. The cars seemed to fly around the tall thin hill.

Soon the diesel came to the first switch. He remembered what the old steam engine had said, and he swung swiftly to the left.

"Clear the way for *meeeeeeee*!" he whistled.

Then, far ahead on the curving track, the big yellow diesel noticed a red caboose swaying along at the end of a train.

"Get off the track, old clickety-clack," he howled.

But the red caboose kept right on going.

"I'll fix you. I'll catch up with you and give you a push," howled the diesel.

The caboose kept right on going.

The big yellow diesel was angry.
He hurried up until he was going
his very fastest. But still, to his
great surprise, he could not catch
that old red caboose.

And then, as if this were not strangeness enough, the big yellow diesel saw a railroad yard right ahead. It looked just like the Tinytown railroad yard.

He saw steam engines standing around watching. They looked just

like the Tinytown steam engines.
   And he saw a man who looked
just like the Tinytown yardmaster
run out and shout, "Stop! Stop,
this minute, you silly fellow! You are
chasing your own caboose around
the tall thin hill!"

The big yellow diesel put on his brakes. He hissed and squealed and finally slid to a stop.

"You played a trick on me," he roared at the oldest steam engine. "You made me go in a circle around the hill."

The old engine was laughing so hard that he couldn't answer for a minute. All the other engines were laughing, too.

"Guess you found someone who wouldn't get out of your way, young fellow," tooted the old engine finally. And he began to laugh all over again at the thought of the big yellow diesel chasing himself.

The diesel thought about it, too.
"Round and round," he thought,
"just like a kitten chasing his tail!"
And then he began to laugh, as
loudly as anybody.

"Gracious me, what a chugging and a tooting and a whistling there is in the railroad yard!" said the ladies in Tinytown that morning.

"That's because a new diesel has come to town," said their husbands. "Sounds as if the other engines are making him welcome."

And, do you know—that is exactly what they were doing!